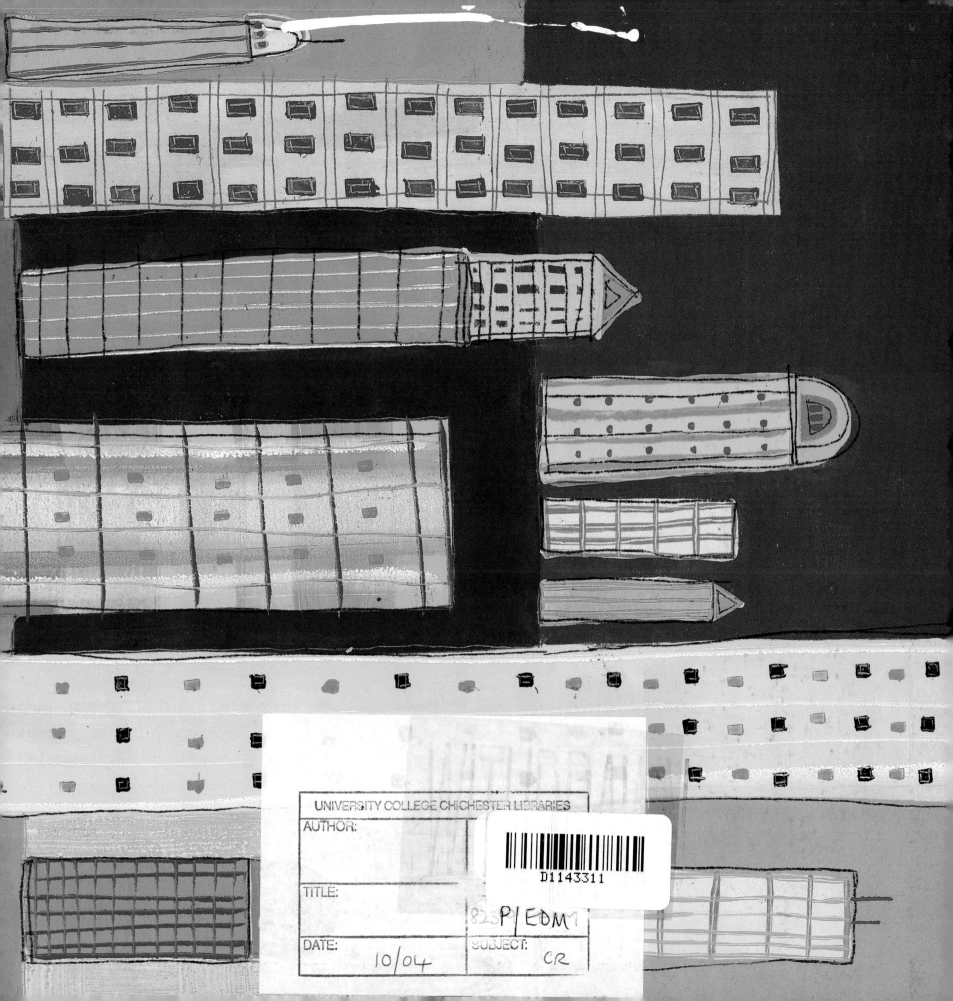

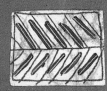

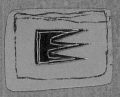

To mum and dad, for making me proud of who I am.
L.E.

For Matthew, with love.
A.W.

AN AFRICAN PRINCESS
A DOUBLEDAY BOOK 0385 60617 6

Published in Great Britain by Doubleday,
an imprint of Random House Children's Books

This edition published 2004

1 3 5 7 9 10 8 6 4 2

Copyright © Lyra Edmonds, 2004
Illustrations copyright © Anne Wilson, 2004

Designed by Ian Butterworth

RANDOM HOUSE CHILDREN'S BOOKS
61–63 Uxbridge Rd, London W5 5SA
A division of The Random House Group Ltd

RANDOM HOUSE AUSTRALIA (PTY) LTD
20 Alfred Street, Milsons Point, Sydney,
New South Wales 2061, Australia

RANDOM HOUSE NEW ZEALAND LTD
18 Poland Road, Glenfield, Auckland 10, New Zealand

RANDOM HOUSE (PTY) LTD
Endulini, 5A Jubilee Road, Parktown 2193, South Africa

THE RANDOM HOUSE GROUP Limited Reg. No. 954009
www.kidsatrandomhouse.co.uk

A CIP catalogue record for this book is available from the British Library.

Printed and bound in Singapore

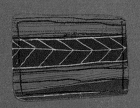

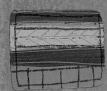

An African Princess

Lyra Edmonds

Illustrated by

Anne Wilson

DOUBLEDAY

My name is Lyra and I am an African princess.

A long time ago a princess was captured from Africa and taken to the Caribbean to live. The princess had many children, who also had children, and soon there were too many princesses to count.

My mama says that we too are part of that story, which has spread far from Africa to every shore.

So when I walk tall in my robe and crown, I am a princess too. Can you see?

At school when they poke fun and say,

"You, an African princess?
Don't be silly!"
"Where's your palace?"

I get very worried that Mama may be wrong.
There are not many African princesses who live
on the tenth floor and have freckles like me.

Mama asks where my crown and fine robe have gone.

"Maybe I'm not a princess at all," I say.

She cuddles me close and whispers, "We'll see."

One frosty day when the windows are all patterns and snakes, Mama shows me some tickets.

"We're going on holiday, to see our African Princess, Taunte May."

At school I can't wait to tell.
Standing on tiptoes I point to the place where my princess lives.

Dad and I make a calendar.

Each night I draw a cross and wish
for the days to go more quickly.

Until one day
when there
are no more
days left.

The door opens on a hot wet world, full of banana trees and humming birds. A new sky wiggles before my eyes and palm trees everywhere wave their friendly arms at me.

I feel the words bubble up inside me and escape my mouth.

"Hello, I'm Lyra. I'm an African princess. Can you see?"

On the savannah where Mama played as a child, a man sings out loud as he chip chops a small hole in a coconut.

"Drink fresh coconut to make you strong like a lion."

We begin to look
for Taunte May on
a hill with a canopy of
guava and sapodilla trees.

"I hope," pants Mama,
"that I can remember
the way."

And I think I can hear
the monkeys giggle
and say, "We know
her, she's an African
princess, tee hee."

Then Mama points ahead, not at a palace, but to a little brown house on stilts.

"Mama, are you sure?" I ask, but she is already tapping on the shutters.

A soft voice calls from within.

Inside it's dark and cool.
I blink and rub my eyes.
There in front of me is an old lady.

No crown or fine robe.
Suddenly all the bubbles
inside me disappear.

Is *this* my African princess?

Then Taunte May smiles and calls me near. She talks of princesses from long ago and princesses around the world, who are all part of my big family tree.

Much later, as we leave,
she whispers in my ear,
"Remember to be proud
of who you are."
And I nod and smile my
happiest princess smile.

Now when they say,
"You, an African princess?
Don't be silly!"

I walk tall and say,
"I'm Lyra,
I'm an African princess.
That's me."